"Oh, no!" I shrieked. On the floor in a corner was Terrible Teddy. He had done it again. Purple eye shadow was all over Teddy's clothes and all over the carpeting. There was even purple eye shadow on our white bedspreads. And that wasn't all! Teddy had used my pink lipstick like a crayon. There were scribbles all over the walls and all over Teddy's face.

Teddy looked up and smiled when he saw us. "Me have fun," he said as he held up what was left of the lipstick.

"Yeah, some fun," I groaned as I glanced at Randi and then at Mom. I could tell from Mom's face that she wasn't going to laugh this time.

DOUBLE TROUBLE

MICHAEL J. PELLOWSKI

cover art by Gabriel
inside illustration by Mel Crawford

Published by Willowisp Press
801 94th Avenue North, St. Petersburg, Florida 33702

This edition copyright © 1994 by Willowisp Press,
a division of PAGES, Inc.
Original edition © 1986 by Willowisp Press

Printed in the United States of America

2 4 6 8 10 9 7 5 3 1

ISBN 0-87406-700-6

To my own double Double Trouble Pack
Morgan, Matt, Melanie & Martin—
and Lucy and Ambrose

One

FIRST off, Randi and I don't think of ourselves as identical ten-year-old twins. I am not a twin. I am Sandi Daniels. I like the colors pink and purple. I like frilly dresses, school work, and romance novels. And I wear glasses, because I'm slightly near-sighted.

My twin sister, Randi, is crazy about sports and the color red. That's why her favorite "dress" is a Washington Redskins football jersey. Her worst subject is spelling, and her eyesight is perfect. Now, does that sound like we're identical?

Of course, we do look exactly alike. We look so much alike I can't stay mad at Randi very long, because—it's like being mad at myself. But I don't get mad at Randi very often. And she doesn't get mad at me. We really are best friends down deep.

However, like I said before, Randi and I are different in as many ways as we are alike. For example, take Sunday nights at our house during the fall. I like Sunday night. It's one night I can sit in the living room and read without being disturbed. It's peaceful and it's quiet. And lately that's a rarity at the Daniels house.

When you have a little brother who is two-and-a-half years old, peace and quiet are things you learn to appreciate. Mom says Teddy will calm down eventually. She says he's going through a stage known as the "Terrible Twos." All I know is, trouble follows wherever Teddy goes as if it were his shadow.

But on Sunday nights even Terrible Teddy settles down. Mom lets him help her clip coupons out of the newspapers. He likes that. And that's why I like Sunday night . . . peace and quiet.

8

Not Randi. Randi thinks Sunday nights are dull. In her own words, "Sunday nights at our house are so boring!"

On one particular Sunday night, I was curled up in an easy chair reading a novel. The story was so romantic! The girl in the story was sick, and her boyfriend was a jerk. I liked the book so much I started crying.

I wiped away tears as Randi walked out of the kitchen and into the living room.

"Where is everyone?" she asked.

"Dad's in the den watching a football game," I answered. "I think Mom and Teddy might be taking a walk."

Randi flopped down on the floor. "Why are you crying?"

I pointed to the book. "This girl has to have an operation. She doesn't have enough money, and nobody will help her," I explained. "You should read this. It's great."

"No, thanks," Randi answered. "Studying soccer plays is all the reading I have time for."

She shuffled her papers and spread them out on the carpeting. "The championship game is just around the corner," she added.

I shrugged my shoulders and turned back to my book. "If you read more books, maybe you'd get better grades in spelling."

"Don't mention that subject to me," Randi groaned. "I just finished my spelling homework." Then she added in a teasing way, "You can be the *A* student in spelling as far as I'm concerned. I'm happy being the star goalie on the soccer team."

I looked up from the page I was reading. "Who cares about sports? Sports make you sweat."

Randi rearranged her soccer plays. "If you worked harder at sports maybe you wouldn't always be the last one picked in gym."

"Big deal!" I replied. "I suppose if we were in the same gym class at school you'd pick me last, too?"

"No, I'd choose you next to last," Randi said, grinning from ear to ear.

"Thanks a lot," I said. "I'll remember that."

"I was just kidding," Randi apologized.

I knew she was. I smiled and went back to my reading.

Just then we both heard a strange noise in the kitchen. It was followed by the voice of our little brother, Teddy. "Uh-oh," we heard Teddy say.

"That sounds like Trouble," Randi said, getting to her feet. Trouble is one nickname we have for our little brother.

I put down my book. "Terrible Teddy is at it again," I answered, using his other nickname. I rose from the chair. "Let's see what he did this time."

Randi and I rushed into the kitchen.

Teddy was standing on a chair near the table. He had an innocent look on his face and his favorite plastic glass in his hand. Lying on the table on its side was an empty container of milk. It had been almost full before Teddy tried to pour himself a drink. The milk was now all over

the table and dripping on the floor.

"I spill moze," Teddy said, pointing at the mess. "Moze" was Teddy's word for milk.

"My homework!" yelled Randi. She rushed up to the table and snatched a soggy notebook from a puddle of milk. "It's ruined! MOM!" she yelled. "Teddy wrecked my homework!"

Both Mom and Dad came into the kitchen. They looked at the mess, and they looked at Teddy.

"I thirsty," Teddy said, holding up his plastic glass. "I want moze."

Mom and Dad looked at each other and started to laugh. Can you believe that? They didn't yell at Teddy. They didn't say a word. They just started to laugh. Milk was dripping everywhere. The place was a mess. And they laughed.

"I don't think it's funny," Randi grumbled, holding up her soggy notebook. "Look at my spelling homework. It's ruined. I have wasted a hour's worth of work."

"We don't mean to laugh," explained Mom.

"But it was just so cute the way Teddy explained it that we couldn't help it."

"Cute?" I said, not believing my ears. "Aren't you going to spank him or punish him?"

"I don't think so," Dad replied. "It was just an accident." He lifted Teddy off the chair. "Come on, Tiger, I'll get you that drink of moze." Dad carried Teddy over to the refrigerator.

Mom took out a roll of paper towels. "I'll get this mess cleaned up."

"What about my homework?" Randi demanded.

"You'll have to do it over," Mom answered. "You shouldn't have left it where Teddy could reach it."

Dad put Teddy down and came over to help Mom. "That's right," he added. "Teddy is still only a baby. You should have put your homework in a safe place when you finished it."

I looked at Teddy. He was gulping down his drink. "There is no safe place with Teddy on the loose," I replied. "He's always in our room."

Randi tried to dry off her homework with a paper towel. "This isn't fair," she complained. "Now I have to do my spelling all over again. And I have soccer plays to study."

Dad was on his knees mopping up milk. He looked up at Randi. "You could use extra work in spelling," he said. "In this house, it's grades first and soccer second."

I was amazed to hear that. Dad was the one who practiced soccer with Randi hour after hour, week after week. He was probably her biggest fan.

Dad continued. "Randi, if your grades in spelling don't improve soon, there'll be no more soccer games."

"Speaking of grades," said Mom, "your grades in gym could do with some improving, Sandi."

"Me?"

"Yes," said Mom. "I talked to Coach Matthews at the game the other day." Mr. Matthews is Randi's soccer coach and my gym teacher at school. "He says you stand around too much in class. He wants you to take a more active part in the games."

I was speechless. All I could do was nod.

"I might as well go to my room and do my homework . . . again," Randi sighed as she stormed out.

"I'll go, too," I said, following my sister out of the kitchen.

Up in our bedroom we sat in silence for a bit. Then Randi spoke. "Terrible Teddy did it again. I love my little brother, but sometimes he gives me such a pain."

I agreed. "Teddy gets away with murder around here just because he's the baby."

"Things were sure nicer before he got into the Terrible Twos," Randi said. She opened her spelling book and began to rewrite her assignment.

"I know," I answered. "It used to be the worst thing that would happen around here was that you'd use one of my favorite blouses

16

to wipe off your muddy spikes. Then 'Trouble' came along," I said, pointing to a picture of Teddy hanging on the wall.

Randi nodded. "That nickname fits Terrible Teddy like a glove," she said. "He messes up the kitchen, and we get a lecture about our grades."

I shook my head in disbelief. "There is no way to figure out parents," I said. "They laughed. I still can't believe it. They laughed."

Randi grinned. "Maybe they'll laugh if we fail spelling and gym and tell them about it in a cute way."

"That'll be the day," I replied. I opened the book I'd carried up from the living room and began to read.

Two

AFTER school several days later, I was waiting for Randi at our usual meeting place. Randi and I always walk home together when the weather is nice. I was getting impatient, because Randi was later than usual.

At last she burst out the back door of the building like the school bully was after her.

"Where have you been?" I demanded.

"Miss Morgan was giving me a lecture about my spelling grade," Randi explained. "I sure wish she hadn't come to our school this year. She's a hard teacher—too hard."

I shrugged my shoulders in response. I really didn't know Miss Morgan that well. But from what Randi and the other kids said about her, I was glad I wasn't in her class.

"Let's go already," I urged as Randi fumbled with her backpack. "I don't want to hang around here all day!" I started off down the sidewalk at a brisk pace.

Randi had to hurry to catch up. "What's the big rush?" she asked. "We have plenty of time to get home."

I began to walk even faster. "I want to stop at the drugstore."

"The drugstore?" shouted Randi, puzzled. "What for?"

"I want to buy something," I yelled back over my shoulder.

"What?"

"If you must know, makeup!" I snapped coldly. Randi froze in her tracks. After a few more steps, I stopped, too. "Well? Are you coming or not?" I asked.

"Mom will kill you!" Randi said. "You know she says we're too young to wear makeup."

"I'm not going to wear it. I just want to buy it."

"Mom won't care," Randi warned. "She'll kill you anyway."

"I have to have it," I told my sister. "The other day I was in the drugstore and saw this great purple eye shadow and super pink lipstick!"

"Purple and pink," muttered Randi, nodding her head in an understanding fashion. "That explains it."

I started walking again.

"You're a dead duck," Randi called after me. "You know you're dead if you do it."

"Mom will never know," I answered. "I'll hide the stuff in our room. Mom will never see it. Now, will you please hurry up?"

Randi readjusted her backpack. She shrugged her shoulders, shook her head, and started off after me.

All the way to the drugstore Randi went on about the makeup. What a nag! You'd think the world were going to end if I broke one little house rule. Besides, I wasn't really breaking a rule. I was just bending it a little.

In the drugstore Randi followed me around and around and didn't say a word. When we passed the newspaper rack, she didn't even stop to browse through the sports magazines like she usually did. Randi was trying to make me feel guilty. But it didn't work. I picked up the eye shadow and lipstick and took it right to the checkout counter.

That's when Randi really embarrassed me. I didn't have enough money to pay the bill. I was twenty-five cents short. "Please loan me a quarter," I whispered to Randi.

"Nope!" she said, folding her arms and shaking her head stubbornly.

The cashier glared at me impatiently. I smiled weakly and nudged Randi with my elbow. "Come on, Randi," I said. "Don't be that way."

Randi smiled and shook her head again.

"Do you want to put something back?" asked the cashier.

"I have the money, thank you," I replied as

sweetly as possible. Then I turned to my sister.

"Give me that quarter!" I demanded. I adjusted my glasses and stared her right in the eye. I looked as mean as I could. She knew I meant business.

Randi exhaled loudly. "All right," she sighed. She dug into her pants pocket. "It's your funeral." Randi slapped a quarter into my outstretched hand.

"Thanks a bunch," I grunted through gritted teeth.

I paid the bill and collected my bag of makeup. Then Randi and I made a hasty exit from the drugstore. "Why did you do that to me?" I grumbled once we were outside. "Everyone was looking at us."

"I just don't want you to get into trouble," Randi explained as we walked away.

"I won't unless someone tells Mom," I answered.

"Don't look at me," Randi replied. "I'm not a squealer."

I stopped. "Thanks for the quarter," I said. I

nudged Randi playfully and stuck the bag of makeup into my jacket pocket.

Randi winked at me in response. "Hurry up or we'll be late," she said. We both started to run. I couldn't wait to get home. I knew I'd feel better when the makeup was safely hidden in our room.

*　*　*　*　*

Mom was busy in the kitchen when we came through the front door. "Hi, Randi, Hi Sandi!" Mom called. "How was school?"

"Fine," we both answered almost in unison.

"Ranee! Sanee!" screeched Teddy as he came racing around a corner. Teddy always gets excited when we come home from school. We dropped our backpacks and took turns hugging and kissing our little brother hello. Arriving home from school was one of the times that almost made Teddy's "Terrible Twos" stage seem bearable. Notice, I said "almost."

Teddy looked at Randi and held up a toy

truck he was carrying. "Ranee play trucks."

Before Randi could reply Mom answered for her. "Randi can't play now, Teddy," she called. "Girls, Dad and I need you in the kitchen. Dinner is going to be late tonight. It's been one of those days. Could you give us a hand, please?"

"We'll be right there, Mom," Randi shouted. Randi handed me her backpack. "Don't you have something to do in our room?" she asked softly.

"Thanks," I whispered back. As Randi walked toward the kitchen, I started up the stairs. "I'll be in as soon as I take our books up, Mom," I called.

Teddy followed me up the stairs. I made him wait in the hall while I went into our room. "Sandi will be right out," I told Teddy as I pushed the door partially shut.

Once in the room I flung our books on the desk in the corner. Then I took out the paper bag with the makeup. I opened the bottom drawer of our dresser and stuffed the bag under Randi's Washington Redskins jersey.

When I opened our room door to leave, Teddy

was still standing there waiting.

"Sandi has to help Mommy," I said as I took Teddy's hand in my own. "Be a good boy and come downstairs with me." I held Teddy's hand as we went down. When we reached the bottom,Teddy plopped down on the last step.

"Me tired," Teddy said as he sat on the step. I left him and went off to help Mom and Dad in the kitchen.

Mom was making a meatloaf, and Dad was chopping carrots for a salad, while Randi was washing leftover breakfast dishes. I went over to Randi, picked up a towel, and started to dry the dishes. After we were finished, Randi and I helped Dad make the salad for dinner.

"Say," Mom said as she slid the meatloaf into the oven, "where is Teddy?"

I stopped cutting the cucumber I was slicing. "I left him sitting on the stairs," I answered. "He said he was tired."

"Maybe he fell asleep," said Mom. "I'd better check on him." She wiped her hands and walked out of the kitchen.

When she was gone, Randi asked, "Did you hide the you-know-what?"

I nodded and began to put tomato slices into the salad bowl. "Everything is under control," I assured my sister. "There's nothing to worry about."

The words were hardly out of my mouth when Mom yelled, "Sandi! Randi! Come upstairs this instant!"

Randi shot a glance in my direction. "Oh, no," I sighed. "What now?" Randi raised her eyebrows questioningly and shrugged her shoulders.

"Randi! Sandi!" Mom shouted again.

"Coming, Mom," Randi answered as she quickly rinsed off her hands. I did the same. Then we both raced out of the room. We thundered up the stairs like a couple of stampeding buffalo.

Mom was waiting in the hall. She looked boiling mad as she pointed through the open door of our room. "In there," Mom said.

Randi slowly eased past Mom into our room. Not me. I was almost afraid to move. I waited until Mom pointed into our room again. Then I finally mustered up enough courage to follow in Randi's footsteps. I stepped in. My eyes opened wide in shock.

"Oh, no," I shrieked. On the floor in a corner was Terrible Teddy. Trouble had done it again. Purple eye shadow was all over Teddy's clothes and all over the carpeting. There was even purple eye shadow on our white bedspreads. And that wasn't all! Teddy had used my pink lipstick like a crayon. There were scribbles all over the walls and all over Teddy's face.

Teddy looked up and smiled when he saw us. "Me have fun," he said as he held up what was left of the lipstick.

"Yeah, some fun," I groaned as I glanced at Randi and then at Mom. I could tell from Mom's face that she wasn't going to laugh this time.

"Where did that makeup come from?" she demanded to know.

I peeked at Randi. Randi pretended not to notice. "I bought it at the drugstore," I confessed.

"Purple eye shadow and pink lipstick," said Mom. "I should have guessed. What is the house rule about makeup?"

Randi answered that question. "No makeup until we're at least thirteen."

"But I wasn't going to wear it, Mom, honest," I quickly added.

Mom walked over to Teddy. She collected what was left of the eye shadow and lipstick. "I wish Teddy felt the same way," Mom said.

"I'll clean it up, Mom," I promised.

"I'll help," volunteered Randi.

Mom tossed the makeup into the wastepaper basket. Then she picked up Teddy. "I'll have to get you cleaned up before dinner, young man," Mom said to Trouble.

"I'm really sorry, Mom," I apologized.

"Sorry isn't enough this time," Mom said. "You'll have to be punished."

I nodded understandably. I was caught. Now I'd have to pay the price. The least I could do was be brave about it.

"Randi has a soccer game after school tomorrow," Mom continued.

"Yes, I know," I said.

"It's an important play-off game," Randi quickly added. Randi was always ready to talk soccer. "All of our friends will be there," Randi continued. "The whole school is going to turn out to support the team."

"I know one person who won't be there," Mom said. She looked me right in the eye. I swallowed hard. "That person will be home babysitting her little brother so her father and mother can enjoy the game in peace."

"Ah, Mom," I complained. "Not that! Staying home is bad enough. Do I have to watch Terrible Teddy, too?"

"Yes, you do!" Mom snapped angrily. She turned and carried Teddy into the hall.

When she was gone, I looked around the

room. What a mess! I thought. What a job it's going to be to clean it up. "Terrible Teddy is a menace," I said as I flopped on my bed. My fingers touched something sticky. I looked at my hand. There was a glob of lipstick on my bedspread. I gritted my teeth and shook my head. "Teddy is two years old. That means two times the trouble," I grumbled.

Randi nodded in agreement. "He's double trouble, that's for sure."

I groaned out loud. "I don't mind missing the game," I began, "but having to watch Teddy is awful!"

"It won't be so bad," Randi replied.

"Ha!" I sighed. "You'll be gone at least three hours. I've never had to watch Teddy that long before." I shook my head sadly. "Besides, he never listens to me like he does you."

"That's because you're not firm with him like I am."

"Firm?" I grunted. "The last time I babysat I told him he was going to sit still while I read him a book or else! You know what he did? He threw a tantrum and screamed for fifteen minutes."

"That's another thing you do wrong," Randi explained. "When you babysit Teddy all you do is read books or play tea."

"Well, what's wrong with that?"

"I always play things Teddy enjoys like trucks or cowboys. You have to keep that kid busy, or he'll drive you bananas," Randi told me.

I got off the bed. "I think it will be the other way around," I said.

"What do you mean?" quizzed Randi.

"He'll keep me busy or drive me bananas."

"Probably," my sister agreed. She bent over and picked up something off the floor. It was her Redskins jersey. "At least he didn't smear lipstick on this." She tossed the jersey over the back of the desk chair.

Slowly, I got up. "We might as well get busy cleaning this up," I said. "Thanks for offering to help."

"Ahh, don't mention it," Randi answered as we went out to get rags and cleaning fluid. "I know if I were in a jam you'd help me."

Randi was right. I would.

Three

THE next afternoon it was Randi's turn to hurry me away from school. She couldn't wait to get home. Randi was riding to the big game with Mom and didn't want to be late. I wanted to take my time getting home. I was in no rush to babysit for Trouble. But Randi wouldn't let me dawdle. She practically pushed and pulled me all the way to our front door.

"We're home, Mom," Randi shouted as we entered the house.

"Hurry and change, Randi," Mom called.

"Right, Mom," Randi shouted.

She ran upstairs while I waited near the door. Mom came around the corner.

"Where's Teddy?" I asked.

"He's on the sofa," Mom replied. "He fell asleep watching cartoons."

My outlook brightened instantly. Could it be true? Did I really luck out? If Teddy stayed asleep even for part of the time, my punishment wouldn't be so bad after all. "I'll let him rest," I said. "There's no sense in disturbing him."

Mom eyed me sternly. "I figured you'd say something like that," she said. Then she smiled and winked. "I'm sure a little extra sleep won't hurt a growing boy," she added.

Just then Randi came galloping down the stairs. She had on her soccer uniform and her lucky red sweatband. "I'm ready. Let's go!"

"Be quiet," I urged my sister.

"Why?" she asked.

"Teddy is sleeping on the couch," I explained.

"Oh," remarked Randi. "Lucky you!" Then she turned to Mom. "Let's go, Mom. Most of the other kids left straight from school with Coach Matthews. I want to get there early, too."

"I'm ready," Mom replied. "I just have to get my purse off the coffee table." Mom walked away.

I held out my arm and shook hands with my sister. "Good luck," I said. "I'm sorry I won't be there to cheer you on."

"Sure. I know you hate watching sports," Randi answered. And she was right. I did. "But I appreciate the thought," she continued. "Besides Dad is getting off early from work. He'll do enough cheering for the entire family."

I agreed. Dad wasn't exactly the quiet type of fan. He always yelled and hollered and got real excited on the sidelines. He was the exact opposite of Mom. She was calm and composed most of the time. She only got excited if Randi did something really spectacular.

Randi glanced at the clock on the wall. "I wish Mom would hurry up," she said.

"Let's see what's taking her so long," I suggested. I headed for the living room. Randi followed.

To our surprise, we found Mom down on

her hands and knees peering under the sofa where Teddy was sleeping.

"What's wrong, Mom?" I whispered.

Mom stopped searching and looked up. "Teddy got into my purse. He took out my car keys. I can't find them."

"Oh, no," groaned Randi loudly. Instantly Teddy began to stir on the couch. I froze and shot an icy glance at Randi. She sighed but kept quiet. Teddy rolled over and fell back to sleep. "Listen, I don't care if he is sleeping," Randi whispered. "We need those keys!" She started toward the couch to wake Teddy. I grabbed her arm and held her back. "Please . . . wait," I pleaded. "Maybe we can find the keys without bothering Teddy," I said. "If we can't, then you can wake him. Until then, please try to be a little quiet."

"Okay," whispered Randi, "but if we don't find the keys in the next five minutes, I'm going to start screaming."

"Girls," ordered Mom, "stop bickering and

start looking. The keys have to be here somewhere," Mom added, crawling toward the easy chair.

We began to search the room. We did it as quietly as possible. Teddy fidgeted a couple times but never opened his eyes. I kept my fingers crossed and looked in every nook and cranny.

Time started to slip by. Where were those keys? I wondered. I began to think the whole thing was a conspiracy on the part of my terrible two-year-old brother. How can anyone be so much trouble even when he's asleep?

I slowly moved across the room I looked by the TV set and near the front window. Randi searched over by the fireplace. Mom was still checking under the furniture. It seemed hopeless.

I dropped down on my hands and knees and peeked under the aquarium stand. Nope! The keys weren't there. Time was just about up. Over near the couch Randi was hovering above Teddy's sleeping form like a vulture. She

was ready to wake him. I only had a minute or two more.

I straightened up and was getting ready to take off my glasses to clean them when I saw the keys.

"They're in the fish tank!" I called in a voice above a whisper. I grabbed the net near the stand and fished for the keys as Mom and Randi joined me. Then slowly, I lifted the soggy key ring out of the water.

Randi's hand shot out and snatched the keys from the net. She flicked a piece of seaweed back into the tank. "Let's go! I'm late already," she said as she turned and marched out of the room.

"Nice work," complimented Mom as she collected her purse from the table. We left Teddy snoozing peacefully on the couch and headed for the front door. It was already open. Randi was outside waiting in the car.

"Hurry, Mom," Randi urged. "Let's go."

Mom paused at the door to deliver some last minute instructions. "We'll be home in a few hours. Take good care of Teddy."

"I will," I promised as Mom walked over to the car and got in. Randi handed Mom the keys, and Mom started the engine. Randi and Mom waved as the car pulled out of the driveway. I waved back.

From the open doorway I watched until our car disappeared around the corner. "This will be a piece of cake," I said to myself as I shut the door. With Teddy asleep I planned to relax and finish my romance novel. This would be more like a vacation than a punishment. It was quiet, and I'd have the house to myself. Well, I'd have it almost to myself. Teddy really didn't count. He was sound asleep on the couch.

Four

I went upstairs to get the book I was reading. When I came back down I decided to check on Teddy before settling in for an hour or so of reading. Quietly, I tiptoed into the living room. I peeked over the back of the couch. What? No Teddy!

"Where did he go?" I muttered. I was slightly startled that he wasn't there. "Teddy? Teddy!" I called anxiously. "Where are you?"

I heard a noise in the kitchen. I raced out of the living room and reached the kitchen just in time to catch Teddy in the act.

Trouble had pushed a chair over to the counter. He was standing on the chair holding a big, plastic bottle of soda. The top was giving him trouble, and the bottle wasn't open just yet. Teddy was so busy struggling with the screw-on cap that he didn't hear me come into the kitchen.

"Teddy! What are you doing?" I cried.

The unexpected sound of my voice frightened Teddy. He turned suddenly and dropped the plastic bottle. The soda bottle hit the floor bottom first. It landed with a loud thud as part of the plastic caved in. The soda began to bubble.

Fizz! The cap cracked as soda began to squirt out. *Woosh!* The bottle exploded! The cap shot off like a rocket launched into space. It would have hit me right in the head if I hadn't ducked. What came next, I couldn't duck.

Fissst! A jet stream of soda came shooting out. "Nooo," I screamed as soda sprayed all over my glasses, all over my blouse, and all over the kitchen. When the geyser finally died down I was half soaked. Pools of soda were bubbling and fizzing everywhere. The kitchen looked like a disaster area.

And as if that weren't enough, Teddy burst out laughing. "Dat's funny," he said as he slid to a sitting position on the chair. "Sanee funny."

"Funny! Funny is it?" I fumed as soda dripped down my face. "I'll show you what's funny after I change out of these soggy clothes." I took off my soda-spotted glasses and wiped them clean with a paper towel. I put them on the counter and walked over to Teddy. I picked Teddy up and carried him out of the kitchen.

When we reached the stairs I put Teddy down on the bottom step. "Now you stay here until I change," I ordered, waving my finger in a threatening fashion. "Don't move. I'll be right back."

I ran upstairs and raced into my room. I left the door open so I could listen for Teddy. I didn't want to leave Trouble alone too long so I did a fast change. "If he blew up the house he'd probably think that was funny, too," I grumbled as I tossed my ruined blouse on the bed.

I needed to throw something on quick.

Randi's Redskins jersey was lying on the desk. I grabbed it and slipped it over my head. I didn't have the time to be choosy.

"Teddy? Are you still sitting there?" I called as I pulled down the jersey. He didn't answer. "Oh, great!" I grunted. I bolted down the hall and thundered down the stairs. Teddy was nowhere in sight. I knew where I'd find him. "Teddy!" I yelled, and headed for the kitchen.

When I got to the kitchen, I found Teddy marching around the room splashing in the puddles of soda. That does it! I thought.

"Theodore Michael Daniels!" I yelled. "Stop that this instant!"

Teddy did stop. He froze right in his tracks. He looked up and stared at me as if confused. Then he blinked once or twice.

"Ranee?" Teddy stammered. "Ranee mad? Me sorry. Sorry, Ranee."

Randi? I thought. What in the world is he talking about? Then the answer occurred to me. Teddy didn't know Randi wasn't home. I

didn't have my glasses on. I was wearing Randi's favorite football jersey. And since Randi and I are identical twins, Teddy thought I was Randi. What a laugh!

I was about to tell who I really was when I thought better of it. Teddy always obeyed Randi better than he did me. I decided to play along.

"Randi is mad," I said. I walked over to Teddy and put him on a chair away from the mess. I took off his sneakers and socks, which were soaked. "Now sit still while I clean up this mess," I ordered.

"Me be good," Teddy said, nodding his head obediently.

"When I'm finished, Randi will read you a book," I added as I began to clean up the mess.

Teddy gave me a funny look. I gulped. "I mean, Randi will play trucks with you," I quickly corrected. Terrible Teddy grinned from ear to ear. "Get out your cars and trucks while I mop up," I said.

"Ho, boy!" cheered Teddy as he hopped off

the chair. He clapped his hands happily and ran into the living room in his bare feet.

I smiled and shook my head. I took my glasses off the counter and put them in their case. I put the case in my pants pocket. "I think I'll keep on being Randi until the soccer game is over," I said to myself as I finished mopping up. "Randi will laugh when she hears about this."

I finished the job and put away the mop. I left the kitchen and went out to get dry shoes and socks for Teddy. I could hear Teddy playing with his trucks in the living room.

"Get ready, Teddy," I called to my little brother. "Here comes Randi!"

Five

TEDDY and I were still playing trucks when I heard a car pull into our driveway. "Stay here. I'll be right back," I said to Teddy. He nodded and started pushing his fire truck around and making siren noises.

I stood up and smiled. For the first time ever, watching Teddy had been a real pleasure— except of course for the soda incident. I couldn't wait to tell Randi about what had happened.

I went to the window. I took out my glasses and put them on so I could see better. The car in the driveway wasn't Mom's. It was Dad's.

I went to the front door and opened it just as Dad reached for the doorknob. "Hi, Dad," I said, greeting my father. "How was the game?"

Dad looked at me and blinked. For a second he didn't say anything. "Hi . . . Sandi," Dad finally answered as he came in and closed the door behind him. "The game was great. We won five to three. Randi had twelve saves."

Dad paused. "Sandi, why are you wearing your sister's football jersey? For a minute you had me confused. I almost thought Mom and Randi beat me home."

"Where are they?" I asked.

"They stopped to pick up some pizzas for supper," Dad replied. He hung his coat in the hall closet and laid his briefcase on the foyer table.

"It's a long story about the jersey," I told Dad. "I spilled something on my blouse and just threw Randi's shirt on for a minute." I decided not to tell Dad about the eruption of Mt. Soda Bottle. I didn't want to have to explain about letting Teddy think I was Randi. Dad might not like it. After all, babysitting Teddy was supposed to be a punishment.

"Where is that little son of mine?" Dad asked. "And how did the babysitting go?"

"Teddy is playing in the living room," I explained. "The babysitting went okay."

Dad started for the living room.

"I want to go upstairs and look for something else to wear," I said to Dad. "I really don't like wearing Randi's clothes."

"Sure, go ahead," Dad said as he walked into the living room. "Hi, Teddy! How's my big boy?" I heard Dad say.

"Da-Dee! Dad!" Teddy squealed excitedly.

Just then I heard another car pull into the driveway. I knew it was Mom and Randi. I started up the stairs. I wanted to get out of Randi's jersey. I was sure Mom would give me the third degree if she saw me in it. And I wanted to keep my little switch a secret from everyone except Randi. After dinner I'd fill her in on all the details.

I dashed upstairs to look for something else to throw on.

* * * * *

Later that night Randi and I held a little private pow-wow in our room.

"You should have been there," Randi said as she rolled over on her bed. "I made this great save on a penalty kick. Coach Matthews said it was one of the best saves he's ever seen."

"You should have been here," I teased. "In fact," I added with a chuckle, "in a way you were."

Randi sat up on her bed. She looked at me in a puzzled fashion. "What do you mean?"

I explained to Randi about the eruption of Mt. Soda Bottle and borrowing her football jersey. When I told her how Teddy thought I was her, Randi laughed out loud.

"And that's not all," I went on. "When Dad came home I had him fooled for a minute or so. If I hadn't had my glasses on, I don't think he would have known it was me."

Randi chuckled and shook her head. "That really is wild," she said. "Imagine Dad and

Teddy thinking you were me. It's outrageous."

"It's not that outrageous," I answered. "If you put my glasses on and wore my clothes, I bet you could pass for me."

Randi got off her bed. "Let's see." She held out her hand. I gave her my glasses. She walked over to the mirror and put them on. I joined her in peering into the glass.

"See," I said. "Now you're Sandi Daniels. And I'm Randi Daniels. I bet we could fool a lot of people."

Randi took off the glasses and turned toward me. "I wish you could be me Monday at school," she said.

"Why?" I asked.

Randi gave me my glasses back. I put them on. "Monday is our classroom spelling bee. I'm always the first one out. Just once I'd like to not be the first person to sit down."

"What do I have to do with that?"

"Everyone knows you're the best speller in school," Randi explained.

I thought for a minute. "To tell the truth, I wouldn't mind if you were me on Monday either. We're having our class basketball play-offs in gym."

"Let me guess," interrupted Randi. "You were picked last."

I nodded. "Nobody wanted me on any of the teams. Coach Matthews' eyes would pop out if I scored a few baskets."

Randi grinned from ear to ear. "Doing better in the spelling bee would also help my spelling grade. I really need to improve, or it's good-bye soccer."

A big smile spread across my face. "Do we dare risk it?"

"What's to risk?" Randi asked. "If you could fool Dad and Teddy, we could certainly fool the teachers at school."

"But what about our friends?" I argued. "They'll figure it out sooner or later."

"Even if they do, they won't tell," Randi said.

She was right, I thought. Even if our friends

did suspect, they wouldn't blab on us.

"Let's do it," I said. "It'll be fun."

Randi nodded. "We can switch clothes in the locker room when we get to school."

"And since gym and spelling are both in the morning, we can switch back before lunch," I said.

Randi and I hugged each other and giggled. We spent the rest of the weekend figuring out the little details of our proposed identity switch. By Sunday night we had all the wrinkles ironed out.

Six

ON Monday morning we arrived at school a little earlier than usual. We carefully avoided all our friends and made a beeline for the girls' locker room. I stood guard in the hall while Randi checked things out inside. In a few minutes the locker room door opened a crack.

"It's all clear," Randi announced. "The locker room is empty. Come on in."

I took one last fast check of the hallway and then slipped inside. Luckily Randi's gym locker was way in the back corner of the room.

"Let's hurry up and change clothes," Randi said as she began to undress.

"And identities," I added, taking off my

sweater and blouse.

I handed Randi my pink blouse and my purple sweater and jeans. She gave me her white turtleneck and her red jogging suit. We switched everything from Randi's red digital watch to my pink socks.

Suddenly the bell rang. "Hurry up," Randi urged as she put on my sneakers and I slipped my feet into hers.

"Done!" I announced as I stood up. "Now for the finishing touch." I handed Randi my glasses.

Randi smiled and put them on. Luckily my lenses weren't too strong. Randi could wear them without much difficulty. "Remember, meet me back here before lunch," Randi said as she checked herself in a wall mirror.

I nodded. We shook hands. "Good luck, Sandi," I said to my sister.

"Same to you, Randi," my sister said to me.

We picked up our books and headed for the hall. We had no sooner opened the locker room door than we bumped into Jamie Collins,

Randi's best friend on the soccer team.

"Hurry up, Randi," Jamie said to me, "or we'll be late for class." I started to snicker as Jamie grabbed my arm and pulled me down the hall. When I looked back at my sister, she was giggling uncontrollably.

"You sure are acting strange today," Jamie said as we turned the corner.

"It's the spelling bee," I told Jamie, trying to sound like my sister, Randi. "It has me all nervous. So if I act a little weird, just pretend not to notice."

Jamie stopped outside of our homeroom doorway. She eyed me suspiciously. "Something strange is going on," she said, giving me a quick once-over. "I don't know what it is, but it's something."

The bell rang again. I smiled, shrugged my shoulders, and went into Miss Morgan's room.

"Good morning, Randi," Miss Morgan said as I passed by her desk.

"Good morning, Miss Morgan," I answered as I quickly went to Randi's seat.

Jamie came in and sat down in front of me. She turned and looked me over one last time. I was sure she knew the truth. I winked.

"That was some game on Friday," I whispered. "How about that save I made on that penalty shot!"

Jamie smiled back. "You were super," she said. Then she turned around to get ready for class.

Luckily nothing much happened through the first hour. I handed in Randi's homework, and we did some math problems. Pretending to be my sister was even easier than I'd expected it to be.

At long last, the moment I'd been waiting for finally arrived.

"Class, now it's time for our spelling bee," Miss Morgan announced.

Instantly a hush fell over the class. Then a buzz of excitement swept up and down the rows as kids cleared their desks for spelling action.

"Everyone will please come to the front of the room, row by row," instructed Miss Morgan. "We'll start with Jamie's row."

We got up and went to the front of the class. Aisle after aisle of kids followed until we were all standing—like prisoners waiting in front of a firing squad.

Miss Morgan picked up her spelling book and took her chair to the rear of the room. She sat down and opened the book.

"Good luck," Jamie whispered. "I hope you're not the first one out. I know how you hate that."

"No talking," ordered Miss Morgan as she looked up. "You all know the rules," she continued. "If you miss a word you have to sit down. The next person has to spell the same word. We'll keep going until we have one class champion."

I gulped and crossed my fingers behind my back. I was second in line. It was now or never.

"Let's begin," said Miss Morgan. "Jamie, spell *adventure.*"

"Adventure," replied Jamie. "A-D-V-E-N-T-U-R-E," said Jamie. "Adventure."

"Very good. Now Randi, spell *emergency.*"

All eyes were on me. My palms felt sweaty. I don't know why I was nervous. Spelling comes easy to me. Nevertheless, I was a bit jittery.

"Emergency," I answered. "E-M-E-R-G-E-N-C-Y," I spelled. "Emergency."

Miss Morgan almost fainted. Her jaw dropped open in surprise. "That's right," she sputtered.

The entire class was amazed. No one could believe their ears. Quickly, Miss Morgan regained her composure. "Excellent, Randi," she complimented. "You must have studied for this."

"I did, ma'am," I said politely. And that was the truth. I always studied spelling. It was one of my favorite subjects.

Miss Morgan smiled and went on to the next kid in line.

Jamie nudged me sharply with her elbow. I looked at her and grinned. She was wide-eyed in astonishment. I shrugged my shoulders, and she smirked smugly as if something had just dawned on her.

The classroom spelling bee continued. Every

time I got another word right, Miss Morgan's amazement grew. She kept looking at me and grinning. It made me a nervous wreck. I couldn't tell if she was proud of me or suspicious of me. I decided not to chance showing off. It was time to miss on purpose and drop out. I'd done well enough as Randi Daniels.

Just then Jamie goofed up the word *Halloween*. She spelled it with only one *L. Halloween* seemed like a good word to go out on.

"Halloween," I began. "H-A-L-L . . . ," I paused and pretended I was thinking.

"Can I start again?" I asked.

Miss Morgan nodded.

"Halloween," I repeated. "H-A-L-L . . . O-W-E-N. Halloween." I grinned, knowing I had left out an "E."

Miss Morgan shook her head. She almost looked disappointed. "No, Randi," she said. "That's incorrect. You'll have to take your seat."

I nodded understandably and tried to look sad. I started to walk to my seat.

As I walked down the aisle I noticed Jamie giving me the eye. As I passed her desk she whispered, "Where are your glasses, Randi?"

I stopped and stared at Jamie.

Jamie winked and gave me a thumbs-up salute. I knew my secret was safe. I smiled at Jamie and eased into my seat.

The spelling bee continued. Sylvia Rumsford ended up winning. Sylvia was a good speller. She was always stiff competition for me at all-school spelling bees.

"Sylvia is our class champion," announced Miss Morgan. "But there are many ways to be a winner." She looked right at me. I tried to slump down in my seat. "Today, Randi Daniels was a winner, too." Miss Morgan continued. "She did better than ever before. Let's give Sylvia and Randi a big hand for their accomplishments."

The whole class began to applaud. They were still clapping when the lunch bell sounded.

"Class dismissed," Miss Morgan announced. Kids got up and began to collect their things from the coat closet. I got up slowly. I wanted to talk to Jamie. But before I could, Miss Morgan called me to her desk.

She waited until the room emptied. "You did a super job today, Randi," Miss Morgan said when we were alone. "It proves that you can do the work."

She reached in her desk drawer and took out a note. As she folded it she continued, "But your excellent work today is not enough to salvage this term's grade. I warned you this might happen."

Miss Morgan handed me the note. It was addressed to my parents. I knew it meant big trouble for my sister.

"In order to pass spelling this semester you'll have to come for extra help every day after school."

"Every day?" I muttered.

"Without exception," she said sternly. "This note explains everything to your parents. Starting tomorrow I'll see you right after school."

I nodded solemnly. Boy! What rotten luck

for Randi. Dad was sure to blow his top. I started out of the classroom.

"Once again, congratulations on your excellent performance in the spelling bee," Miss Morgan called as I went out the door.

Putting the note in my pocket I raced down the hall to the locker room. Since everyone was in the cafeteria, the hall was deserted. I opened the locker-room door and sneaked in. I found Randi at her locker.

"Where have you been?" Randi demanded. "I was getting worried. Hurry up and get my clothes off."

I started to change. I wanted to get back into my own stuff, too.

"How did it go in gym?" I asked as we swapped sneakers.

"It went perfectly," Randi replied. "Coach Matthews almost swallowed his whistle when I picked up a loose ball and swished one through the basket."

"You didn't overdo it, did you?" I asked as I

dressed in my own clothes.

"Nah," answered Randi. "I scored about ten points." Randi paused and smiled at me. "But I couldn't resist scoring a basket against Billy Parker. He thinks he's such a hotshot jock."

"No one suspected that you were me?"

"Well, some of your friends found me out," Randi said. "I just couldn't fool them. But they didn't squeal. By the way, how did I do in the spelling bee?"

"Great!" I told Randi as we tied our shoes. "Miss Morgan was really impressed. But . . ."

"But what?" cried Randi. "What's wrong? Did you get caught?"

I shook my head. "Jamie Collins knows about the switch, but Miss Morgan never suspected."

"Then, what's the problem?"

I took out the note and handed it to Randi. She read it as we walked out of the locker room.

"Oh, no," she groaned as we walked down the hall and headed for the cafeteria. "When Dad reads this, my soccer career is doomed!"

Seven

RANDI was in a state of shock as we entered the lunchroom.

"That was a great shot you made today in gym," Billy Parker called to me as we walked by his table. Billy Parker had never even spoken to me before. It made me feel good even if it was Randi who made the basket.

I smiled and waved in acknowledgment.

"How'd you learn to play so well all of a sudden?" Sidney Green asked as we walked past the lunch line. Sidney was a nerd who had a crush on me. He was always following me around. I couldn't stand him.

"It just came naturally," I said as I brushed

by him and guided Randi toward our usual seats. Randi was in a daze. She bumped into Sidney and almost sent his lunch tray flying.

"Sorry, Sidney," I quickly apologized.

"Yeah, sorry," Randi repeated.

"Ah, it's okay," Sidney replied as we hurried away.

Kids kept shouting comments to us as we weaved in and around tables and chairs. We both got lots of compliments we really didn't deserve. The select few who knew about our switch laughed every time anyone said something nice about Randi's spelling or my basketball playing.

At long last we reached our usual table which was in a corner of the lunchroom.

"What's wrong with Randi?" Jamie Collins asked as we sat down. "Isn't she thrilled about doing so well in the spelling bee?" Jamie teased.

Randi shot Jamie an icy stare.

"What did I say?" Jamie muttered.

"Spelling," I explained.

"Spelling?" quizzed Jamie. "That's why Randi is walking around like a zombie?"

"Read this," Randi said to Jamie. She handed over the note. Jamie read it and whistled.

"That's bad news," she sighed. "After school every day with Miss Morgan? That explains your semi-conscious state."

"That's not half of it," I added as I opened my milk and unwrapped my ham sandwich. "She has to start tomorrow—no exceptions. That means she can't play for the community soccer team anymore."

Jamie almost choked on her peanut butter sandwich. She gagged and coughed. I slapped her on the back. "I didn't think of that," she sputtered when her throat cleared.

"And the championship game is this week," moaned Randi. "While the team is playing for the title, the goalie will be in Miss Morgan's room studying spelling."

Jamie took a deep breath and exhaled loudly. "There are a few days until the game.

Maybe you can talk Miss Morgan into letting you off that one day. She might understand."

"Fat chance of that," grunted Randi. "Miss Morgan is all books and no sports. She doesn't know the difference between a soccer net and a fish net. And she could care even less."

Jamie nibbled on a chocolate chip cookie. "How about your dad?" she asked. "Won't he let you off? He loves soccer. And after all it *is* the championship."

Randi chewed on a pretzel stick. She looked like she was eating her last meal. "No way," she grumbled. "You don't know my dad."

"Around our house it's grades first and everything else second," I said as I slurped my milk. "Besides, Dad just warned Randi about her spelling grades. I doubt if he'll take her side."

We were all quiet for a few minutes. What else was there to say? I finished my sandwich and unwrapped my snack cake. "Aren't you going to eat your lunch?" I asked Randi.

"Starving yourself won't help."

Randi made a sour face. "Nothing will help at this point," she said sadly. "To solve my problem I'd have to be in two places at once." She leaned over the table and rested her chin on her arm.

Suddenly, a big smile flashed across her face.

"That's it," shouted Randi. She snapped into an upright position and grinned.

"Uh-oh," I muttered as I swallowed hard. "I know what you're thinking."

"What?" quizzed Jamie. "What are you two talking about?"

"She wants to be in two places at once," I explained. I turned to Randi. She still had that silly smirk plastered on her face. "If anyone finds out, we'll be in big trouble," I warned.

"Will you two tell me what's going on?" Jamie demanded.

"There'll be two Randi's and no Sandi," my sister told her pal, "like today in spelling."

Jamie's eyes lit up like Roman candles. "Hey! That might work," she said. "You guys fooled Miss Morgan once. I bet you can do it again."

"But will Sandi risk it?" Randi asked. She and Jamie looked at me.

What could I say? How could I refuse? My sister was in trouble and needed help. I knew how important that game was to her. And I knew if the shoe were on the other foot, she'd fill in for me.

"You know I'll do it," I answered.

Randi and Jamie bear-hugged me between them.

"Hold on a minute," I said. "What about Mom and Dad? We at least have to give them a chance. Maybe they will help Randi."

"I'll show them the note," Randi said. "If they tell me I can't play soccer, then our consciences will be clear," she said. "We can't let the team down."

"Yeah! Think of the team," Jamie said to me.

"Okay," I agreed. "I guess no one will get hurt if I become Randi Daniels one more time." I turned to my sister. She was unwrapping her lunch. "I thought you'd lost your appetite."

"It just came back," Randi said, taking a big bite of her sandwich.

Eight

THAT night after dinner, the entire family was in the living room when Randi handed Dad the note. Randi and I watched in silence as he read it. He didn't look happy, to say the least. When he finished he showed the note to Mom. She read it and then looked at Randi. Dad was already staring at Randi, too.

Randi fidgeted in her seat on the couch. "Well, someone say something," she said softly.

"You'll have to go for extra help every day after school. That means soccer is out," Dad told her.

"But, Dad, what about the championship?" asked Randi. "If I go for spelling help, I'll miss the title game."

"Yeah, Dad," I quickly added, coming to the aid of my sister. "What about the championship?"

"What about it?" Dad asked, as if he didn't know what we were talking about.

"What bout it? What bout it?" Teddy mimicked as he started to bounce on the cushions of the love seat.

"Stop that, Teddy," Mom ordered. She went over and picked him up. Then she sat down and held Teddy on her lap. "Now what about the game?" she asked.

"If I go for extra help every day I won't be able to play in the title game," Randi explained. "Could you talk to Miss Morgan about letting me out at least for that one day?"

"It's only one day, Dad," I pleaded. "The team needs Randi. Think of the team!"

Dad looked at me. "Randi, will you please tell your lawyer to rest her case?"

Randi turned toward me and raised her eyebrows. I bit my lip and sat back in my seat. We both knew the decision of Judge Daniels was about to be rendered.

"Granted, it's only one day," said Dad. "But, Randi, you've been repeatedly warned about your spelling grades. Every time you get in trouble, we can't get you out of it."

Dad paused, then continued. "Grades are your responsibility, Randi. You're the one who has to pay the price for your own actions."

Randi scratched her head. "That means I can't go to the game?"

"I'm your biggest fan," Dad went on. "I'd love to see you play in that game. But the answer is no. You have to do what your teacher says, championship or no championship."

Randi folded her arms and sighed loudly. She looked me right in the eye. I knew she was thinking *I told you so.*

"But what about the team?" I asked. "You're letting the team down."

"Da team! Da team!" Teddy cried.

Mom shushed him. "The team will have to do without Randi," Mom said. "We don't like this any better than Randi does. But as parents, we have to make decisions that sometimes seem harsh or unreasonable. Someday you'll understand why. Being a parent isn't always easy."

"Well, I guess that's that," Randi said coldly as she stood up. I did likewise. Randi walked out, and I followed her.

"I'm sorry, Randi," Dad called after us.

His apology did little to improve our moods. Randi was mad at our parents. I was disappointed in them. They didn't even try to see our side of it. At least that's the way it seemed to us.

When we got to our room, Randi shut the door. "There's no other way out now," she said. She walked over to her bed and sat down. "You have to go to spelling for me."

"I said I would, and I will," I told her. "I just don't like fooling Mom and Dad. But I know how important this game is."

"I don't like fooling them either," Randi said. "But it's kinda like when you bought that makeup. You didn't deliberately disobey to hurt anyone. You just had to do it."

I nodded as I opened my notebook and began to do homework. I thought about the makeup incident. Boy! That sure backfired.

"No one will ever find out," Randi promised. It was almost as if she'd read my mind. "I'll get excused from soccer practice. I won't tell Coach Matthews about going for extra help. So when I show up for the game he'll never suspect anything."

I shook my head. "I don't know. It sounds risky to me. Suppose Coach Matthews and Miss Morgan get together. They work in the same school, you know."

Randi leaned over and picked her soccer ball up off the floor. She laid back on her bed and spun the ball in her hands. "Don't sweat that," she said. "They don't talk the same language. Matthews is a jock. And you know about Miss Morgan. Opposites never talk to each other, not even in the faculty room."

"I hope you're right," I said. "But we'd better plan this out carefully so there are no slipups."

Randi agreed. "There's a lot of time before the game. We'll plan out every little detail," she said.

*   *   *   *   *

During the next couple days, that's just what we did. Jamie helped us hatch our little plot. She was the only one with whom we shared our "Operation Double" scheme.

When we were done I had to admit everything looked perfect on paper. On the day of the game I'd tell Mom I had to work on a report at the school library so she wouldn't expect me at home. Randi would put her soccer uniform in her gym locker. Then after school Randi and I would meet in the girls' rest room to switch clothes. We couldn't use the locker room this time because the team would be in there.

Once we swapped identities, I would go to spelling, and Randi would go to the locker room as Sandi. That's where Jamie came in. She would stand guard while my sister changed from my clothes into her uniform. Then Jamie and Randi would ride to the game with Coach Matthews and the rest of the team.

The second part of the plan covered switching back. After spelling I'd hide in the girls' rest room until the team returned. When the coast was clear, Jamie would bring me into the locker room. Randi and I would dress in our own clothes and go home.

Nine

ON the day of the game everything was all set for Operation Double. As soon as the final bell rang, I made a beeline for the girls' rest room in the back hall. We'd purposely picked that room because it was close to the locker room and wasn't used after school very often.

I checked the hall before I pushed the door open. It was all clear. There wasn't a soul in sight. I went in. Randi was waiting near the sinks.

"Let's go. Hurry up," she urged.

"Right," I answered, putting down my books.

We went into adjoining stalls and began to change. We passed each other articles of clothing under the stalls. In a few minutes the transformation was complete. We stepped out and faced each other.

I took off my glasses. "You won't need these," I said. "I'll keep them with me just to be safe."

Randi nodded. "It's a good thing you only need them to see far away," she said.

"Yeah," I replied, "or Randi would have a heck of a time studying spelling words without them."

Randi smiled. Then she gave me a big, long hug. "Thanks, Sis," she said. "You don't know how much I appreciate this."

When she let go I winked at her. "Yes, I do. Now let's get going. You have a game to win."

Randi nodded. "You'd better go first," she suggested. "I'll wait until you're gone, and then I'll sneak into the locker room. Jamie is standing watch there."

"Good luck," I called as I paused at the door. Then I walked out. I turned to walk to Miss Morgan's room. Suddenly I froze dead in my tracks.

"It can't be," I gasped. My eyelashes batted nervously. Walking right toward me were Miss Morgan and Coach Matthews. They were smiling and chatting like a couple of long lost pals.

"There she is now," Miss Morgan said as she pointed at me.

"Randi Daniels! You're just the girl we want to see," Coach Matthews called.

My mouth dropped open. I was at a loss for words. My brain said, "Run for it, kid!" But fear nailed my feet to the floor.

As Miss Morgan and Coach Matthews approached, I heard the girls' rest room door creak open behind me. Then I heard it bang shut. I was on my own. The world wasn't ready for two Randi Daniels.

"Randi," began Miss Morgan as she put a hand on my shoulder. "Why didn't you tell me about the championship game?"

I looked from Miss Morgan to Coach Matthews and from Coach Matthews to Miss Morgan. "I . . . I . . . ," I blubbered. No words came out.

"Relax, Randi," said Coach Matthews. "When you missed practice, I knew something was funny. Today I asked around and found out about the extra help you were getting."

"Who told you? Jamie Collins?"

"No," replied the coach. "It was Billy Parker."

"Great," I mumbled. "Just great."

"I went to see Miss Morgan," Coach Matthews continued. "As it turns out, Margaret, I mean Miss Morgan, is a big soccer fan."

Miss Morgan smiled. "I played on my college team as a mid-fielder," she said. "Since I don't live in town, I didn't know anything about the community league until today."

I was totally confused. None of this was part of the plan. I felt like I was trapped in a room with no way out and the walls were closing in.

"What it all boils down to is this," said Coach Matthews. "You don't have to go for extra help today."

"I don't?" I cried in total disbelief.

"Of course not," Miss Morgan stated. "One

day more or less won't make much of a difference. Besides, the team needs its star goalie."

Coach Matthews beamed. "Isn't that great news?"

"Wonderful," I said as I forced myself to grin weakly.

"But there's no time to waste," the coach continued. He began to usher me down the hall toward the locker room. "You have to hurry and change. Do you have your uniform at school or do I have to call your home and ask your mom to drop it off?"

"Uh, my uniform is here," I answered quickly.

"Good," he said. "But I'll call your home anyway. I'm sure your parents will want to see you play today. Won't they be surprised?"

I nodded. "They'll be surprised if I play today," I said. And boy did I mean it!

We were at the locker room door. Coach Matthews' office was right across the hall.

"Go in and change your clothes while I

phone your Mom," the coach instructed. "I'll wait right here until you come out."

"Good-bye, Randi. Good luck," said Miss Morgan as she walked away.

"Thank you, ma'am," I said as I went into the locker room. It was deserted.

I found Jamie sitting on a bench near Randi's locker. When she saw me, she stood up. "Sandi?" she whispered. "Is that you?"

I nodded.

"What are you doing here? Where's Randi?"

"She's dressed in my clothes and stuck in the girls' rest room," I replied.

Jamie looked puzzled. "She'd better get in here and fast," Jamie cried. "The team is in Coach Matthews' van waiting to leave."

"Randi can't get in, and I can't get out," I explained. I quickly told her what had happened. "And," I added, "Coach Matthews is waiting outside. He's calling my mom right now."

"We're doomed!" sighed Jamie. "What are we going to do?"

I eyed Randi's soccer uniform. Jamie had laid it out on the bench. "What can I do?" I replied. "I have to get dressed and go to the game. If I don't, everyone will know about the switch. Then we'll really be in trouble."

"But what about the game?" Jamie asked. She gulped and added, "You can't play goalie!"

I started to put on Randi's uniform. "I know I'm not a very good soccer player," I admitted. "But I've played goalie in gym class a few times, and I know most of the rules from going to the games. I'll just have to do the best I can."

Jamie nodded understandably. Neither one of us uttered another sound as I dressed. What was there left to say?

"I'd better take these," I said to Jamie once I had Randi's uniform on. I picked up my glasses and tucked them into my top pocket. Together Jamie and I walked toward the door.

Coach Matthews was waiting when Jamie and I came out of the locker room. "Hurry up, girls," he said as he took us down the hall.

"Randi, I got in touch with your mother. She's going to call your dad. They're all driving to the game after they find your sister. She's at the library or someplace." The coach hurried us down the hall. "I'd look for Sandi myself to give her the message, but we're late already."

We walked by the girls' rest room. My sister isn't in the library, I thought. She's closer than you think.

As we passed the girls' rest room, Jamie nudged me with her elbow.

"Coach, can I use the girls' rest room before we leave?" I asked.

"We're really late, Randi," Coach Matthews replied as he ushered us toward the exit. "You're just nervous. You can use the facilities at the field. It's only a short drive."

Before I could argue or stall he opened the outside door. His van was parked near the exit. "Let's go," he said as he led us to the van.

The rest of the team was already in the van. Jamie and I got in. I sat down and didn't say a word. Several kids on the team stared at me in shock. Randi's uniform didn't fool them one bit. They knew I was the wrong Daniels twin. The van began to buzz with whispers. Soon everyone except Coach Matthews knew who I really was.

Good old Jamie saved my skin. She went from seat to seat explaining my predicament. When the kids heard the story, they all looked at me and smiled. Everyone kept my secret. What a great bunch!

"We're off!" Coach Matthews said as the van pulled away.

I looked out the back window as the van drove off. I saw a girl standing in the parking lot watching us leave. It was Randi.

Ten

RANDI had heard almost everything from her hiding place in the girls' rest room. As soon as the van left, she wasted no time in heading for home. In fact, she ran all the way.

When she reached the house, she was practically exhausted. Randi opened the door and stepped in.

She bent over to catch her breath. "I'm glad you're home, Sandi," Mom said when she saw her. "It saves me the trouble of stopping at the school library for you. Hurry and change your clothes. We're going to see Randi play for the championship."

Randi straightened up. Mom's face registered

shock. "Sandi! I mean Randi! Randi? Which one are you?"

"I'm Randi," my sister admitted breathlessly. She sighed deeply and owned up to the truth. Randi knew it was no time for excuses. Quickly, she told Mom everything.

Mom couldn't believe her ears. She was mad, but not too mad to chuckle a little about the stunt we'd pulled off.

"Your father was glad to hear that Miss Morgan had allowed you to go to the game," she told Randi. "He's on his way there now. But he might feel differently when he finds out about this."

Randi told Mom she'd accept any punishment Dad and Mom decided to dish out. She also admitted that it was all her fault. That was a nice touch on her part

"We'll worry about blame later," Mom told her. "Get on something you can play in while I dress Teddy. Sandi will be counting the minutes until we arrive."

Randi went up and threw on sweatpants and her Redskins football jersey. It was a good choice since the team's soccer uniforms were red, too. She grabbed her old soccer spikes and ran back downstairs.

Teddy was dressed and ready to go. But Randi couldn't find Mom. "Randi," she heard Mom call. "Help me. Teddy took the car keys again. He doesn't remember where he put them. Help me look for them."

Randi began to search the house. Of course the first place she looked was in the fish tank. But she had no luck this time. The keys were nowhere to be found.

At long last, when all seemed hopeless, Mom remembered something of value. "I used to have a spare key to the car," she told Randi. "Now where did I leave it? I haven't used it in ages."

"Key? Key? Mommy key?" Teddy said.

"Yes, we're looking for Mommy's keys," Randi said to Teddy. "Where are they? Do you remember now?"

Teddy raced off into the kitchen.

"You don't suppose he remembers now?" Mom asked Randi.

Randi shrugged in response. Then they raced off after Trouble. They found him in the kitchen near the back door. He was pointing at the key rack.

"Keys!" he kept repeating.

"Teddy's a real help as usual," Randi grumbled.

Mom stepped up to the rack for a closer look. It was amazing! The spare car key was there! That's where she'd left it. "Let's go," Mom shouted to Randi as she snatched the key from its peg.

Quickly Mom hustled everyone out the back door. As she did she muttered, "For Sandi's sake, I hope we're on time."

Eleven

AS far as I was concerned it was already too late. With Jamie's help I'd managed to bluff my way through the warm-ups and pre-game drills. But now I was out of time. The game was about to begin, and I didn't know what to do.

I certainly couldn't fake playing goalie. During pre-game shots, I'd missed a lot of balls. Luckily, Coach Matthews attributed my clumsiness to pre-game jitters. He didn't guess I was really Sandi Daniels, the kid always picked last in gym.

Suddenly a whistle sounded. Both teams started to line up for the official check of spikes. Only rubber spikes are allowed. As I stood with our team, Jamie came over to me.

"I'm going to tell Coach Matthews the truth," I said as the official passed us. "It's not fair to the team to keep this up any longer."

"Stop worrying," Jamie said. "The team talked it over. Everyone, even Billy Parker, is behind you one-hundred percent."

"What?" I answered in astonishment. "You guys want me to play?"

"That's right," Jamie assured me. "We want you to play goal until Randi gets here. We really don't have a back-up goalie anyway. We'll do everything we can to help you out."

The officials finished checking spikes. The teams started toward opposite sidelines for last-minute instructions from their coaches. Boy, was I nervous. The championship game was about to begin, and Randi was nowhere in sight. I was actually going to have to play goal. What a predicament!

I swallowed hard and walked toward our bench.

"Good luck, Sandi . . . I mean, Randi," Billy

Parker said. He winked and trotted past. The other kids also wished me well as we walked off. It made me feel good inside. I actually felt like part of the team. I just wished my knees would stop shaking.

"In here, team," Coach Matthews called. He drew us into a circle for a little pep talk.

"We worked hard all season for this," he began. "This is the most important game we've played so far this year. And the team we're playing is a very good team."

Coach Matthews turned to look right at me. "They are going to score goals," he said. "We'd love a shut-out, Randi, but don't get upset if they put the ball in the net."

He looked around at Jamie and the other kids. "The defense has to help Randi. And our offense has to score. We can win it, team. Let's do it!"

Coach Matthews stretched out his hand. Everyone put his or her hand on top. Soon there was a pile of hands. I put my hand on, too.

"WIN!" Everybody shouted as we broke from the huddle.

Jamie and I trotted out onto the field together. She gave me some quick pointers on what to do. I also remembered a few things from gym class and from watching Randi play. Thinking about Randi was what worried me the most. My sister really was a star goalie. I knew I couldn't play half as well as Randi could, but I sure planned to give it my best shot.

The whistle sounded. The opposing team kicked off. "Who has the ball?" I shouted to Jamie as players bunched up around midfield.

"Can't you see?" Jamie called without looking back at me. She positioned herself to my left.

"Not really," I answered. "The middle part of the field is kind of bleary." Just then I spotted the ball as it sailed high in the air toward the other team's goal.

Jamie relaxed and looked back at me. "I forgot about your glasses," she said.

"I could put them on," I answered.

"I have them in my pocket."

"You'd better not," Jamie warned. "If Coach sees you in glasses, he'll know something's fishy."

Suddenly a loud cheer went up from our side of the field. Jamie and I turned. We saw Billy Parker running toward us with his arms in the air. Other players were mobbing him.

"We scored," Jamie shouted as she ran up to congratulate Billy on his goal.

"Way to go, Billy!" I shouted. Was that me? I wondered. I couldn't believe it. I'd never been excited about sports before. I'd never really cared who won or lost. But this was different, somehow. It was a new feeling. And I liked it! I wanted to win!

The whistle blew again. The other team kicked off. I squinted and tried to follow the ball as it bounded from player to player.

"Uh-oh," I muttered as the opposition moved the ball down the sideline toward me.

"Be ready," Jamie shouted as she ran out to meet the charge.

Jamie went toward the player with the ball. He passed to a girl with long blond hair. She was all alone running full speed right at me. There was no one to defend against her. She took the pass and dribbled in on goal. It was me against her.

I got ready. This was my moment of truth. The blond-haired girl kicked the ball. The shot was on target. I tried to knock the ball away but missed. It rocketed past my outstretched hands and into the net for a score. Boy, did I feel terrible.

Jamie quickly ran up as the official took the ball out of the net. "It wasn't your fault," Jamie said as she patted me on the shoulder. "Don't feel bad. That girl is Sharon Smith. Her nickname is Sure Shot. She's the leading scorer in the league."

Billy Parker came running over. "You tried your hardest," he said. "Don't let it bother you. The game is far from over."

But it did bother me. It bothered me a lot. The score was tied. I didn't care if that Sharon girl was the top scorer in the league. I didn't want

her to score any more goals. Right then I made a decision.

I reached into my pocket and took out my glasses. I put them on.

"Randi!" yelled Coach Matthews from the sideline. He waved at me to get my attention. "Don't let that goal get you rattled." Then he stared at me in a funny way. It was the glasses. He kept looking at me as if he couldn't believe his eyes. "Randi, is that you?" he called.

I pretended not to hear.

"Since when did she start wearing glasses?" I heard him shout to the kids on the sidelines.

"Since right now," Jamie Collins muttered as she walked down the sidelines and got back into position. Jamie smiled at me.

I nodded at Jamie, and then I turned to look over to the sidelines. I waved a salute to Coach Matthews. I was ready to play.

The whistle sounded, and we kicked off. I could see clearly now. Billy Parker took a pass in the middle and broke into the open. He dribbled toward the net and fired a hard shot. The opposing goalie caught the ball and kicked it out to a teammate.

I was so busy watching the action on the field, I never noticed that my dad had arrived. He took his usual place on the sideline right by Coach Matthews.

"What's the score?" Dad asked the coach.

"We're tied at one a piece," Coach Matthews replied.

Dad surveyed the field. "I'm really glad Miss Morgan excused Randi from spelling," he said. Dad looked over at me. It was then that I spotted him, too. I waved.

"Randi? Is that Randi?" he muttered. "No! That isn't Randi. It's . . . no, it can't be. Can it?"

"What do you mean it's not Randi?" Coach Matthews cried. "Sure it is! Isn't it?"

"It's not Randi," a lady said. Dad and Coach Matthews turned. Mom, Randi, and Terrible Teddy had arrived at last.

Teddy saw me out on the field and smiled.

He pointed. "Sanee! Sanee!" he shouted. "Sanee play soccer!"

Coach Matthews glanced at Randi and then at me. Dad looked from me to Randi.

"I'm confused," Dad admitted.

"Me, too," Coach Matthews added as he doffed his cap and scratched his head, looking puzzled.

Out on the field I didn't have time to be confused. That blond girl, Sharon Smith, had stolen the ball from Billy Parker. She was speeding down the field. All that stood between Sure Shot and me was Jamie Collins.

Jamie tried her best, but she was no match for Sharon Smith. Sure Shot dribbled around Jamie and left her far behind. Once again it was a one-on-one matchup.

Sure Shot teed up the ball and fired a bullet. It looked like a sure goal. But I saw it coming in plenty of time to react. I moved to my right and dove, stretching as far as I could. I got my hand on the ball and grabbed it. I held it tightly as I went tumbling to the ground.

"What a save!" shouted Coach Matthews as the spectators began to applaud. Slowly I got to my feet. My ankle felt sore. I had twisted it slightly making the save. I hobbled back toward the goal.

The official blew his whistle. "Injury time out," he shouted. "You'll have to put a new goalie in," he called to Coach Matthews.

I took off my glasses and tucked them back into my pocket. I began to limp across the field to our bench. Every one of my teammates gave me a high five. What a feeling! It was the greatest.

"Substitute time," I called as I stepped over the sideline. "Randi Daniels for Randi Daniels."

"Are you okay?" asked my sister, looking at my ankle.

"I'm fine. Really! It's nothing," I assured everyone.

Randi smiled and ran out on the field.

"Two Randi's?" Coach Matthews mumbled. "Am I seeing double? What's going on?"

"It's a long story," Mom said to Dad and

Coach Matthews. "We'll explain later."

"One thing is already clear to me," Dad replied. "There is only one Randi. She's in goal now." He put his hands on my shoulders and squeezed softly. "The young lady who just made that super save is my daughter, Sandi."

"Sanee! Sanee!" shouted Teddy as he gave me a hug.

I put on my glasses and hugged Teddy back. Then I picked him up and held him in my arms. I pointed at Randi who was already doing a super job in goal. "Let's watch the game," I said to my little brother.

And what a game it turned out to be! It was a seesaw battle all the way. Sharon "Sure Shot" Smith had several good shots on goal. But she didn't score again. Randi managed to block every shot. Randi was just outstanding. Many of her saves were nothing less than phenomenal.

I guess Randi's performance in goal inspired the rest of the team. They never let up for a second. With less than a minute to play, the game was still tied one to one. Then we got lucky. Billy Parker was fouled and awarded a penalty kick. He kicked a beauty. His shot caught the upper corner of the net. The opposing goalie was helpless. We went on to win the championship by a two-to-one score.

After shaking hands with the opposition, the team mobbed Coach Matthews. I was one of the mob. When we all settled down, he congratulated us on our victory.

"You all did a great job," he complimented. "Billy, you were outstanding." Then he looked at Randi and me. We were standing side by side.

"Even when the score was tied, I knew we'd win," Coach Matthews teased. "They didn't stand a chance against our secret weapon."

"What secret weapon?" Jamie Collins asked.

Coach Matthews pointed at Randi and me. "Our goalies," Coach said, "the Daniels twins, Randi and Sandi. They had everyone baffled . . . even me."

We all laughed. Then the parents and fans

began to applaud. Our mom and dad clapped the loudest. I felt like I was going to cry. In fact I did. I looked over at Randi. Tears of pride were rolling down her cheeks, too. I guess twins are alike in more ways than they sometimes admit even to each other. What a great feeling!

Twelve

THAT night at dinner, the Daniels family held a private victory party at home. Mom cooked a Chinese dinner. Dad bought a gallon of our favorite ice cream for dessert. And Terrible Teddy accidentally showered the victors with a spoonful of peas.

"Now about this switcheroo you two pulled . . . ," Dad said to Randi and me as he glared across the table at us. "You were lucky things turned out all right. But if you ever switch identities again, there might be big trouble," he warned sternly.

"We've had enough double trouble, Dad," Randi assured him "We promise we won't do any more switching."

"That's right," I agreed. "We'll never switch identities again. I want to be Sandi Daniels all the time."

"And I want to be Randi Daniels all the time," my sister added. She winked at me and smiled.

"I still think you deserve some kind of punishment," Mom said as she wiped ice cream off Teddy's face. What a sloppy eater Teddy was. He even had ice cream in his hair.

"I agree," Dad added. "And I know just the punishment." He smiled at Mom. "For the next two Saturday nights the girls will have to babysit Teddy while we go out to dinner."

"I like that," Mom said. "It sounds fair."

I agreed, and so did Randi.

"Well, I hope you girls learned a lesson from all this," Dad said.

"Oh, we did," Randi replied as she spooned ice cream out of her dish. "I learned that even the best plan can backfire," she joked.

"And I learned that I really like sports,"

I said. "Soccer is a lot of fun."

"Bravo!" applauded Dad. "What amazes me the most about this whole mess is that Coach Matthews asked Sandi to join the soccer team as the back-up goalie."

"Yeah!" Randi said. "Coach says we made a dynamite combination in net. We're double trouble for the other teams."

Mom nodded. "Just remember, Miss Dynamite," she said to Randi, "you have to get your spelling grades up."

"I will," Randi promised. "I'm going to work extra hard from now on. Coach Matthews is going to talk to Miss Morgan about working out a schedule so I can practice and get help in spelling, too." Randi flashed Mom her best smile.

"And I'll help," I volunteered. "Spelling is easy once you get the hang of it."

Dad finished the last of his dessert. "Well, it sounds like the perfect happy ending," he said.

"YEAH!" yelled Teddy as he began to clap.

SPLAT! He knocked over his milk glass.

"I spill moze," Teddy cried as milk ran all over the table. We all jumped up and grabbed paper towels to stem the flash flood. Mom righted Teddy's glass as we quickly soaked up the rivers of white liquid.

"I thirsty," Teddy said holding up his now empty glass. "I want more moze . . . moze from the frigafrator." He pointed at the refrigerator.

"I'll get it," I said as I tossed my soggy towels in the trash. I went over to the refrigerator and opened the door. I took out the plastic jug of milk. Behind it I spotted something that didn't belong.

"Hey, this story really does have a happy ending," I announced. I reached into the refrigerator and took out Mom's missing car keys. "Look what I found. Teddy hid Mom's car keys in the refrigerator."

"In frigafrator!" Teddy yelled.

Everyone looked at Teddy. Trouble just smiled.

About the Author

Michael J. Pellowski was born in New Brunswick, New Jersey. He is a graduate of Rutgers, the state university of New Jersey, and has a degree in education. Before turning to writing he was a professional football player and then a high school teacher.

He is married to Judith Snyder Pellowski, his former high school sweetheart. They have four children, Morgan, Matthew, Melanie, and Martin. They have one cat, Kitty, and two cocker spaniels, Spike and Brandie.

Michael has written more than 125 books for children. He is currently writing scripts for a popular comic book series. When he's not writing books, Michael enjoys fishing with his family as well as jogging and exercising.